Fun with Fortune Cookies

Are you tired of boring fortune cookie messages? How many times have you broken open your cookie to find a dumb saying like, "All your dreams will come true" or "Good things come to those who wait"? You'd have more fun staring at the fish tank in the Chinese restaurant than reading *those* fortunes!

With the *Fantastic Fortune Cookie Kit*, fortunes are as wild and wacky as you always dreamed they could be. Haven't you always wanted to tell your little brother that his room is really a portal to outer space? If you tell him in a fortune cookie, he just might believe it! But you don't have to use our fortunes. You can make up your own crazy fortunes, too! Cut colored paper into small pieces. Then write your own fortunes on the papers. Fold or roll the fortunes so they can fit inside your cookies. Fortunes can be cheery, silly, mysterious, or even mischievous! You can bring fortune cookie valentines to school on February fourteenth, or make fortune cookie April Fools' jokes on April first!

Where Do Fortune Cookies Come From?

Are fortune cookies an ancient Chinese custom? Did famous Chinese philosophers like Confucius write the very first fortunes? Probably not! Actually, fortune cookies were invented in the United States! But there is a legend that fortune cookies came from a Chinese tradition:

During holidays and festivals in medieval China, one tradition was to exchange special moon cakes made from lotus-nut paste (kind of like peanut butter). In the thirteenth and fourteenth centuries, the Mongols invaded China and took control of the Chinese government (Mongolia is a country north of China). But the Mongols didn't like lotus-nut paste. The Chinese knew their enemies wouldn't eat moon cakes, so they got the idea to store secret messages inside the cakes!

When the Chinese were planning a revolt against the Mongols, they wrote their secret plan on tiny slips of paper. They hid the papers inside moon cakes and handed them out to people. Thanks to these little "fortunes," the attack was successful. After this, people started putting messages inside the cakes just for fun. This story may or may not be true, but it adds an exciting twist to the history of fortune cookies!

Attack at dawn tomorrow.

Fortune Cookie Fun Facts

- Fortune cookies first became popular in the U.S. when the Chinese settled in San Francisco during the gold rush.
- Police in the U.S. and Hong Kong have used fortune cookies to spread anti-drug messages.
- Fortune cookies were first made by machines in the U.S. in 1964. Before that, they were made by hand.
- Now you can get fortune cookies in Chinese restaurants all across America, Canada, and Europe!

How to Make Your Own Fortune Cookies

Here is what you will need:

Equipment:

large bowl
measuring cups and spoons
eggbeater, electric mixer, or fork
plastic spoon or teaspoon
well-greased cookie sheet
hot oven
spatula
tray or cutting board
oven mitts
fortune cookie molds
fortunes

Never use an oven without the help of an adult. Always use oven mitts.

Ingredients:

4 tablespoons (60 ml) butter, softened
$\frac{1}{3}$ cup (.08 l) sugar
2 egg whites
$\frac{1}{4}$ teaspoon (1 ml) salt
1 teaspoon (5 ml) vanilla extract
$\frac{1}{2}$ cup (.12 l) all-purpose flour
$\frac{1}{3}$ cup (.08 l) water

Directions:

(Makes 15 cookies)

1. Make sure you have all your fortunes handy and ready to go!

2. Have an adult preheat the oven to 375°F (190°C).

3. In a large bowl mix the butter and sugar with an eggbeater, electric mixer, or fork until they are fluffy. Then add the egg whites, salt, and vanilla extract. Beat until everything is smooth. If you use an electric mixer, be sure to have an adult help you.

4. Stir in the flour and water.

5. With the spoon, scoop out an even spoonful of batter. Carefully pour it onto the well-greased cookie sheet. Use the back of the spoon to form a circle about 3 inches ($7\frac{1}{2}$ cm) in diameter. The batter should be very thin, almost transparent. Do not pour more than three circles onto the baking sheet at a time. You will have to work quickly to shape the cookies before they harden.

6. Have an adult put the cookie sheet in the oven. Bake the cookies for about 7 minutes, or until the edges begin to turn golden brown. Do not overcook!

7. Have your adult helper take the cookie sheet out of the oven. Using a spatula, remove one cookie from the cookie sheet and place it upside-down on a flat surface such as a tray or cutting board. You now have about 1 minute of working time before the cookie hardens. This is more time than you think!

8. Place your fortune in the middle of the cookie.

9. Very gently and loosely, fold the cookie in half over the fortune. The cookie will be warm, so try to touch only the edges.

10. Next, pinch the two ends together, folding the cookie into the shape of a fortune cookie.

The oven, as well as the cookie sheet and cookies, will be hot! Be sure to have an adult help you with the rest of these steps.

Hey! Try These Yummy Twists!

Have you ever had a chocolate fortune cookie? What about a green one? Surprise your friends with your own unique fortune cookie inventions!

- ✆ To make chocolate fortune cookies: Add 1 teaspoon (5 ml) of cocoa powder to the flour.
- ✆ To make orange fortune cookies: Add 1 teaspoon (5 ml) of orange extract or $\frac{1}{2}$ teaspoon ($2\frac{1}{2}$ ml) of finely grated orange rind to the batter.
- ✆ To make fortune cookies in your favorite colors: Add 2 drops of edible food coloring to the batter.

11. Turn the cookie on its side and place it in the cookie mold to keep it from coming unfolded. Leave the cookie in the mold until it hardens, usually about 2 minutes. Meanwhile, move on to your next cookie. If the remaining cookies harden before you have a chance to fold them, pop them back in the oven for 1 minute.

12. Repeat steps 5 through 11 until you have used all the batter. This should make about 15 cookies.

Fantastic Fortune Ideas

rd of a *misfortune* cookie? This can be a great way to play a joke
misfortune cookie can say something like:

dog will eat your homework tomorrow.
TV will break during your favorite show.

If you want to be really creative, you can try writing messages that rhyme. You
could be the Shakespeare of fortune cookies! Rhyming fortunes can go like this:

- If you eat this cookie and play your cards right
  You can watch TV until midnight tonight!

- Your science teacher won't be so mean
  If you do all your homework and scrub the
  boards clean!